Betty Hagen

The Gift of the Dove

The Gift of the Dove

BETTY HAGER

Illustrations by
Catherine Reishus McLaughlin

ZondervanPublishingHouse
Grand Rapids, Michigan

A Division of HarperCollins*Publishers*

The Gift of the Dove
Copyright © 1991 by Betty Hager

Requests for information should be addressed to:
Zondervan Publishing House
1415 Lake Drive, S.E.
Grand Rapids, Michigan 49506

Library of Congress Cataloging-in-Publication Data

Hager, Betty.
    The gift of the dove : a parable for Christmas / Betty Hager.
      p. cm.
    ISBN 0-310-54690-7 (pbk.)
    1. Christmas stories. American. 2. Parables. I. Title.
  PS3558.A32318G54 1991
813'.54—dc20   91–16552
                                                   CIP

Cover Design by Terry Dugan

Printed in the United States of America

91 92 93 94 95 96 / AM / 10 9 8 7 6 5 4 3 2 1

The Gift of the Dove

Chapter One

"Poor little dove," the other doves said. "His mother and father have been caught in snares. Ah, he is so young to be without parents."

The terrible news confused him. He had been asleep when the dove neighbors returned to the stable. His mother and father had left early in the morning to forage for grain, and they had been gone a long time. All day he had awaited their return.

He yearned for the warmth of his mother

holding him snugly in their nest above the rafters. He longed for her gentleness, the caring touch of her beak as she preened the feathers on his neck. He craved the pigeon's milk stored in her craw.

The doves tried to comfort him.

"Of course it will be hard, little one, but you must always remember it is an honor to be chosen. Your parents will be sold as sacrifice in the Holy City. You must not grieve."

He must not grieve? Why, he had not yet learned to fly. His mother had given him his first lesson that very morning before she left. He had not yet learned to search for grain, nor did he know where the wild peas grew. He couldn't imagine life without his mother. All day he mourned.

But the following morning something happened that gave him hope. He heard the sweet strains of a song, not unlike the soft cooing of his gentle mother. He craned his skinny neck to find the source.

A dove neighbor said, "While you were quite small and your mother was teaching you the lessons of survival, a Child was born in the stable

below. We heard his birth cry. His Young Mother coos to him."

This small person created in him a new life. He looked below, and his eyes met the eyes of this Child. A miracle lay in the infant gaze; the instincts of the turtle-dove surged anew in him. He would eat the food his dove neighbors brought to him for strength! He would live!

He wanted to be close to the Child, and learning to fly was the answer. It looked easy enough. He watched the other doves leave their perches with little effort. They lifted with freedom, wings twisting and flattening as they rose.

He would try that. He crawled to the edge of the next perch, his heart pounding. The dirt floor seemed far away. With his spindly legs he pushed, but he had not noticed how the other doves quickly brought their legs back to their bodies. With frenzied swiftness he flapped, attempted to check his fall, but it was useless. He was unable to keep from sprawling upon the swaddling clothes of the infant in the stall below.

The Young Mother turned to the Tall One at her side.

"Husband!" she cried. "This young dove fell on our baby! Our little one could have been hurt!" She suddenly stopped. "Oh, the poor little dove! Please see if it's all right."

The Tall One lifted the dove and examined him closely.

"He doesn't seem to be hurt."

With care he closed his big hand around the dove, then climbed across the bars of the stable posts until he reached the rafters, carefully returning the bird to his nest.

When he climbed down, he said to the Young Mother, "Poor little Tor-yonah," using the Hebrew name for turtledove. "Perhaps I should move the manger so it won't happen again."

"Ah, such a pretty dove," the Young Mother said. Her voice was soft. "You're certain he wasn't hurt?"

The Tall One smiled. "He was more startled than our baby."

The dove thought, *I'll be all right, and I'm glad I didn't hurt the Child, but I wish I could be near him. Hmmm. Tor-yonah. My name is Tor-yonah.*

The next day, Tor-yonah again tried to fly.

He lifted his toes into the air and drew his thin legs close. His wings swept down, then up to the sun, and he flew!

He flew cautiously about the olive trees, joyously past the acacia bush, and mischievously under the legs of the donkey that grazed near the stable doors. It seemed to him that the Child's gaze followed him wherever he flew.

In the days that followed, Tor-yonah watched the family, and learned of kindness and love. But when the stableboy kicked a lamb, he was troubled. He decided he had much to learn about the world of people.

There was something different about this particular family of people. Especially the Child. A brilliant star gleamed with a bright intensity over the stable. There were visitors who came to see this baby—lowly shepherds and rich rulers who brought gifts. They said a star had led them there.

Tor-yonah felt a bond with the Child. He sensed his love. He would serve him. This little boy would be his master. He knew the Child was his reason for being. He was not many days older than the Boy, but he soon realized that doves develop more rapidly than people. Even so, there was little he could do to serve. With his beak he lifted the cloths that covered the baby, and tucked them closely around the infant's small neck and shoulders.

The Young Mother smiled, but she sighed, "Gently, Tor-yonah. Gently, please."

He understood her feelings, remembering his own mother's protecting wings. But he wanted to show the Young Mother that he'd bring no harm to her baby.

The rulers had brought sweet-smelling gifts. He searched the courtyard until he found a winter primrose. With his beak he snipped the flower and laid it before the Child.

The Young Mother laughed—she couldn't help it. "He's too young for that, Tor-yonah. He could choke on the petals."

She placed the flower behind her ear; he liked that.

"If I didn't know any better," she said to her husband, "I'd think this little bird was trying to give our baby a gift."

"That sounds like something you'd believe," the Tall One chuckled. "I could remove the nest, but we must leave for home as soon as we return from our visit to the Holy City. By then he'll probably fly away."

Tor-yonah grieved. He didn't want them to leave! He had adopted these people for his family. He wanted them to adopt him! He would stay away from the baby. Maybe he would learn how to please them. He kept to his nest but closely watched the Child.

On the tenth day of Tor-yonah's new life the family arose and left before the sun brought its light and warmth to the stable. He had heard them talk of "cleansing rites" in the Holy City. All through the morning he fretted about them, and when the sun had gone to its home and the family had not yet returned, he was listless with worry; he couldn't bear losing another family. He knew with certainty that he would die if this happened. Sleep didn't come until their late-night return.

The following evening he heard the Young Mother sing a song that started him on his quest for a gift again. The words told of the Most High Lord who had created the earth and all its creatures. He listened carefully. She sang of a good man long ago. The Most High told the good man that he was going to send a swelling water upon the land because the people had not obeyed him.

She is singing of Yahweh, Tor-yonah thought, and even in his thoughts he felt awe and reverence at that sacred name. When the husband or wife spoke of the Great Lord, they whispered. Even in song the Young Mother whispered his name.

She sang of how the good man was to build a house that would float upon the waters. He was to take with him all his family and two of every living creature. Tor-yonah leaned so far to hear the words that he almost fell from his perch.

The Young Woman's voice rose as she sang of how the Most High caused the waters to form upon the face of the land, and all who disobeyed were destroyed. Her voice sweetened as she sang of the wind that passed over the face of the earth, how the waters ceased, and how the fountains of the deep and the windows of heaven were closed.

Then Tor-yonah heard something that was to him as his mother's stroking beak. She sang of a *dove*. He wanted to hear more of that. He flew to a closer perch. His heart leaped within him when she sang, "And the dove came back, the dove came back, the dove came back with an olive leaf!"

She placed the baby in the straw. The Child slept soundly, and the Young Mother danced as she swept the stable floor with a cornstalk broom.

Tor-yonah thought, *A dove! She likes that part about the dove and the olive leaf. She dances and smiles. The leaf and the dove have special meaning for her.*

He flew back to his perch. Now he knew what to do about the gift. It would be a gift that would show he was a part of this family. A gift to seal the bond between him and the Child. A gift that would show his solicitude for the Young Mother and the Tall One. The first thing in the morning he would get a leaf—no, a branch—from the ancient olive tree that grew outside the stable door. His toes curled in a sleep-grasp on his perch, and he slept.

When he awakened, it seemed that the olive tree inclined its silvered branches toward him. The Young Mother and the Tall One were asleep on their bed of hay. The baby slept too, but Tor-yonah saw the first early morning stirrings: a puckered face and tiny fingers seeking a rosy mouth.

He lifted his legs in a joyous leap and flew straight to the tree. There was a slender branch almost as long as his body, its leaves moist with the dew of morning. He twisted and tore with his beak. The distance was short, but the size of the branch made flying difficult. Struggling for balance, he flew back through the open doors.

The Young Mother had awakened. She was leaning over the manger. Tor-yonah placed the branch at the baby's feet. With a sharp sigh, the Young Mother closed her fingers over the branch. Tor-yonah hovered near.

She is frowning. She doesn't like the gift.

But she cried out to the Tall One, "Are you awake? You must see this! Tor-yonah has brought our baby an olive branch!"

Still holding the olive branch, the Young

Mother gathered the baby to her. With tenderness she slipped the fingers of her other hand around Tor-yonah. As she sank to her bed of hay, she held the dove close to the Child.

"Ahh, Tor-yonah, you are a special gift of the God of gods for our baby, I'm sure of it."

She was quiet as she nursed the little one, and when she whispered, "Little dove," Tor-yonah knew it was for both of them. At last he had the love and warmth he had been seeking, but he remembered the Tall One's saying that they must soon leave the stable and return to their home.

Surely now they will keep me forever, he thought. *Surely now they will take me with them when they go.*

Chapter Two

The star was halfway across the heavens, and a shaft of silvered light shone through the stable doors. In a darkened corner the Tall One and the Young Mother lay sleeping on the hay. With amazing suddenness, a light far brighter than the star surrounded the man. Startled, Tor-yonah awakened and saw that the man too had awakened.

"What is it?" the Tall One asked, bewildered.

An urgent voice said, "Get up! Take the

Child away from the king of this province to the land of the pharaohs. He is searching for your son and has made plans to kill him!"

The light faded as swiftly as it had come. The Tall One sat up, holding his head in his hands. Tor-yonah could feel the Tall One's hopelessness weighing on his own heart. After a while, the man touched the Young Mother's face gently. She opened her eyes.

"An angel of the Lord God has come to me in a dream. We must go. Our baby's in danger here."

Tor-yonah watched his family get up and make preparations to leave. It was as if they had been visited by angels before. The Young Mother held her baby with protecting arms; denarii were left for the innkeeper, and the donkey was untethered. Their few belongings were tied to his back, and the Young Wife was lifted to sit among the bundles. A sling of cloth was tied across her chest, and the infant was placed there over her heart.

The dove thought, *They aren't going to take me.*

But then the Young Mother said, "Come,

Tor-yonah," and she patted her shoulder to show where he might perch. In his haste he almost flew past her, teetering as he landed.

"Shh, shh," she whispered when the baby murmured.

The cobbled streets of the town softened under the starlight. The family moved with caution along back alleys and streets.

"Where will we go, Husband?" the Young Woman whispered.

The Tall One looked about to see if others might be lurking near.

"Do you remember my speaking of a kinsman who moved many years ago to the land of the pharaohs? The one who trades in wood—fir, cedar, and cypress? It is the season for his caravan to pass along the Great Sea. I hope to travel with him."

Because the angel had urged them to hasten, they walked through the night. In the morning, shining before them, was the Great Sea. Somehow the sight of it lessened their fears.

"How beautiful it is!" the exhausted Young Mother said. "Could we stop on its shores to break our evening's fast?"

"I'd like that," the Tall One answered, "but first I must find a friend of my youth who lives in the town below. He will know when my kinsman passes through."

Tor-yonah hoped to go with the Tall One. The night's journey from the stable had been his first great adventure. When morning had dawned—when other birds were chirping and the roosters had crowed their welcome to the day—he had flown from his perch, soaring high into the heavens. He had been the first of the family to glimpse the Great Sea. Far to the east where the sea curved to meet the land, pastels washed across the sky— grays, blues, pinks, and lavenders—and close to the water a bright slash of orange shouted the coming of the sun.

At his birthplace he had seen his reflection in a courtyard pond. The pastels were the colors of his feathers, and when he had lifted his wings, there, underneath, was the color of the reflected sun. He was proud that Yahweh—the Most High—had chosen to give his skies the colors of a turtledove.

The family stopped at a hillside cave overlooking a grove of almond trees. There was a carob tree beside the cave.

"We can pick the brown pods and shuck the seeds for the donkey," the man said.

The girl saw hyssop growing on the cave's outer walls.

"And look—zufä. We'll pick the leaves. The taste of it on bread is pleasing."

She hastened to remove the flour from their packs, hopeful to show him the home-loving skills her mother had taught her.

"If you will draw water from the stream there—and choose a few smooth stones for baking, I will make bread while you are gone."

The Tall One brushed a strand of hair from her forehead. "Once we are away from the evil king's grasp, I will be certain your needs are met forever."

When he had drawn the water and found the stones, he climbed up on the donkey. Before he moved downhill toward the town, he placed a hand to her cheek.

"Watch with care. Stay close to the cave, and keep the baby hidden."

When Tor-yonah heard that, he knew he would not go with the Tall One. He must guard the Young Mother and the little boy.

After the Tall One was gone, the girl pulled long grasses and made a bed in the cave. For a while she and the baby slept. When she awakened, she made a fire and prepared the bread, flattening the round cakes of it between her hands before baking them on the hot stones. She gathered carob pods for the donkey's return. Tor-yonah was given seeds from a pouch.

The woman was young, but Tor-yonah had never seen her at play. The innkeeper's daughters, not much younger than she, had chased one another in the courtyard. On this day she chased Tor-yonah about the open space near the cave, laughing in the untroubled tones of a girl. The sky was a clear, clean blue, and the sun was bright. For a while her fears were forgotten.

The sun had moved but a short span in the sky when Tor-yonah heard the sound of a horse along the rocky path that led to the cave. The Young Woman must have heard too, for she hastened to hide, but it was too late! A large,

burly man reined his horse to an abrupt stop when he saw her. Tor-yonah flew to the carob tree by her side.

With admiring eyes, the Horseman looked at the girl.

"My, what have we here? I can't believe my eyes. What's a pretty young woman doing in the hills above town at this time of year? It's certainly too late for almond harvest."

His eyes narrowed.

"All alone, eh? But how did you get here? You've run away from harsh parents, maybe?"

The Young Mother was silent.

"Hmmm," the Horseman mulled. "There are many tiring miles to walk to the town below. Have you come here from the south?"

Tor-yonah was proud of the Young Mother. A moment before she had been a child, but now he could see shining in her proud eyes the woman she was to become. She lifted her chin high and returned the man's gaze with candor.

"I am traveling with my husband, sir. I expect his early return."

The Horseman looked at the Young Woman

for a long time. The earth was still. The breezes of
early morning seemed to stop with their breath-
ing. Suddenly the air was rent with the sharp
hunger cry of the Child. The Young Mother
paled. She ran quickly toward the cave.

"Stop!" the Horseman commanded.

In shock the girl turned back to him.

The man's voice softened, "You have a child
. . . I didn't know . . . This morning I rode from
the south. The king has decreed that his soldiers
kill all male children under the age of two. I've
never seen anything like the carnage. If the child
is a boy, I suggest you leave this place as soon as
your husband returns."

Tor-yonah was hurt to see the fear in the
Young Mother's face. He flew quickly to the tree
close to the cave.

The Horseman paused for a moment. With a
quick jerk he spurred his horse.

"Shalom!" he called back.

The Young Mother leaned in weakness
against the tree.

She whispered, "Shalom."

When the Horseman was out of sight, she

rushed to the Child. Her long, uneven sigh as she cradled the boy told Tor-yonah how frightened she had been. He flew to her. They did not leave the cave until afternoon when the sounds of the donkey were heard outside. Then they both flew (each in his own way) to the mouth of the cave.

The donkey's packs were bulging, and from the Tall One's black beard a white smile flashed.

"We are blessed. My friend has found a tent for us. And he's given us dates, figs, and fresh cakes from his wife's baking. And listen to this! My kinsman passed through here only two nights ago. We should be able to catch up with them; cargo slows their caravan."

Something in the Young Woman's face must have made him stop.

"Why, what's wrong? Is the baby ill?"

He stepped down from the donkey, and the Young Woman rushed into his arms. Trying hard to hold back the tears, she told him of the Horseman.

"I was sure he was going to hurt me, but the God of our fathers was here. When the baby cried, he changed his mind."

"I should never have left you alone," the man said.

The incident with the Horseman had made them cautious again. There was no time to break bread by the shores of the Great Sea. The donkey was fed. The husband and wife ate their bread and zufä as they walked. The Tall One had filled their flask with goat's milk at the home of his friend, and they passed this between them.

With only a donkey for transportation, they were unable to hurry. They plodded on.

The man limped now, and the girl insisted they change places for a while. When she turned her head away to hide a gentle smile, Tor-yonah thought it must be because of the tenderness in her husband's large hands as he held the baby. Tor-yonah flew above them, keeping his eyes on the road but always watching the family. Every joy, every fear of the family was his. When it was almost dark, he discovered something that he must tell them! He flew down to them with excitement. He swooped sharply past the Young

Mother's head and circled the donkey. He sailed toward the Tall One's nose and quickly curved away before he made contact, twisting and flattening his feathers as he gained altitude.

The man stopped the donkey and looked around, perplexed.

Tor-yonah immediately descended to hear what they might say.

"Tor-yonah's gone mad," the Young Mother laughed. "What can be wrong with him?"

The man laughed too. "I almost believe you are right about that dove. He seems to be trying to tell us something."

"Don't treat him lightly," she said. "There's a reason for his being here."

Then her hand went to her mouth in fright. "You don't suppose he's seen the soldiers, do you?"

"Not likely," the Tall One said, but Tor-yonah saw the apprehension in his eyes.

They labored on, the man walking again, the sleepy Young Mother trying to keep her eyes open so that she and the baby wouldn't sway and fall. Tor-yonah watched from his shoulder perch. He wished there were some way he could tell them what he had seen.

The sun drifted out of sight below the sea, and Tor-yonah saw the land had become flat. The road skirted vast marshlands, and after a while, even in the starlight the sea was no longer visible. They were traveling inland.

"I'm certain we're near the border now," the Tall One said. "Once we've crossed it they can't harm us. But there are other dangers. There may be robbers along the way."

Tor-yonah was alarmed when he heard soft weeping sounds. He had not heard the Young Mother cry. He was relieved when the man stopped the donkey, lifted his wife down, and held her in his arms.

But in a moment the man drew back.

"Listen! I believe I hear the sounds of music and the voices of men. It may be our caravan. Perhaps that was what Tor-yonah was trying to tell us."

Tor-yonah lifted his head. It was about time the Tall One believed in him!

"Praise be to the Great Shepherd, our Lord!" the Young Mother cried.

"I join you in praise," the husband agreed, "but we must still be cautious."

"Why? Won't your cousin be pleased to see you?"

"Ah, yes, but this may not be his caravan. Even if it is, we must not risk being mistaken for those who would prey upon them. I'm going to hide you and the baby in the reeds. I'll be back for you soon."

He smoothed a place for them and laid the donkey's saddle blanket upon it. When the Young Mother lay down with the Child, he arranged a robe over them and covered it with marsh grass.

"Try to sleep. May the God of Abraham protect you."

Tor-yonah saw the wide eyes of the Young Mother shining in the dark for a long while. He heard her whispered prayers to Yahweh. Time seemed suspended in the air around them, unmoving—a dark and fearful cloud. Eventually the Young Mother joined the Child in sleep, and although Tor-yonah tried to stay awake, he too must have slept. He was awakened by the welcome voice of the Tall One.

"My cousin! I want you to meet my lovely wife, my wonderful son, and . . . ," he added, laughing at the dove nodding nearby on a piece of driftwood, "and this is Tor-yonah. He's part of our family too."

"Shalom!" the man with the Tall One said.

The Young Mother sat up, rubbing her eyes with her fists. The Child awakened too. Tor-yonah cooed as he pushed aside the dreams of the warm stable.

They looked into the black-eyed, red-bearded face of the kinsman.

"Shalom to you, sir," the Young Mother said, and Tor-yonah hoped his "coo" would also be understood as *Shalom.*

Chapter Three

Later, when Tor-yonah
came to know the kins-
man, he believed all their problems were solved.
He liked the gruff yet tender man who attended to
the comforts of this family. Now the Child would
be safe. Tor-yonah would watch over him as
closely as ever, but they were pleased to know
their larger needs would be met.

It did not occur to him he might have reason
to fear for his own safety.

When they joined the caravan, Tor-yonah

experienced his first separation from the Child. The kinsman had his servants set up tent for the family. After all the arrangements were completed, he came into their tent.

"You seem troubled, Cousin," he said to the Tall One.

"I am," the Tall One said. "I don't know how to provide for my family in this new land."

"Do not fear," the kinsman said. "Are you not a carpenter like your father, Heli, before you? I can set you up as a maker of wooden farm implements for the farmers of the area. There's a great need for the tools of farming in my land— plowshares, yokes, spades for digging. I can supply you with good hard fir for your carpentry business."

"May you be blessed for your kindness," the Tall One said.

Then the kinsman told them of an ancient fig tree that grew beside the Blue River. His home in the City of the Sun was on the other side of the river, not too great a distance away.

"We'll set up tent for you there beneath its protecting branches. Your labor will be longer than the passing of the day, for many farmers will soon come to you."

With gentle hands he picked up the dove. "My servants will bring you food, and I will take your dove to the livestock area for the evening."

The Young Mother smiled a tender smile.

"Tor-yonah may stay with us."

"He will cause no problem for us," the man said. "I will see that he is given food and water."

Tor-yonah heard the Tall One protest, but the kinsman evidently did not, for he walked from the tent, crooning to the dove. The man's kindness was no help, for Tor-yonah felt an almost physical pain at being separated from the Child. When he kept the other animals awake with his crying coo, one of the servants who watched over the goats, sheep, donkeys, and horses said, "Sometimes a bird needs it eyes covered; perhaps the light from our fire is disturbing. I'll make a tent with my robe and cover him."

He knew the servant acted in thoughtfulness, but he hated not being able to see. The darkness only made his worries seem greater, and he did not sleep until he was returned to the family in the early morning.

One evening the kinsman forgot to come for Tor-yonah, and the dove soon knew why. The caravan had set up camp for the night, and the people gathered around a great fire. Musicians came with lute, harp, and pipe, and the music lifted the hearts of the weary travelers. Tor-yonah watched the Tall One and the Young Mother as they joined the others in a sacred, swaying dance of their people. On the tent pole where he perched, the dove moved and danced in his own way to the ancient melodies.

The journey to the land of the pharaohs took several days, and each night the kinsman sent his servant for Tor-yonah. Tor-yonah dreaded the setting of the sun, when he would be taken to the livestock area. He fretted throughout the nights and was greatly relieved when the caravan arrived at the fig tree.

The kinsman had his servants set up tent for the family and left supplies. Then he bid them good-bye.

"When you are settled, I will send a servant to bring you to us for the Sabbath. My family will be pleased to know their relatives from the Town of the Branch."

And when the kinsman turned to the Young Mother, Tor-yonah was surprised to see tears on his ruddy cheeks.

"My wife is like that virtuous woman of the sacred scrolls; she laughs at the time to come. But she's a woman of warmth, and she will draw you and the Child to her like the brooding duck along the shores of the Blue River. There's something about you and your baby. I don't know . . . Something . . ."

He mounted his horse and rode to rejoin the caravan.

For a while Tor-yonah felt secure. This man would be a trusted guardian for his family; he held them in esteem. And Tor-yonah also felt safe because he was free to come in and out of the tent at will. Wherever the Child was taken, Tor-yonah followed. By the shores of the Blue River he watched over the little one while the Young Mother washed clothing on the rocks. He perched near him while she made bread in the outdoor oven. When the Child slept, Tor-yonah found a place among the leaves where he might look down upon him. The Child was ever in his line of vision, for he had an uneasy feeling that their next separation would be permanent.

When not many days had passed, an incident occurred that troubled him. On the Sabbath, the kinsman sent a servant in a small chariot to take the family to his home. When the carriage arrived, his wife and children rushed out to greet their relatives. According to custom, the children kissed their own hands in respect for their guests. There was much laughter and joyous confusion. The kinsman led the way through the courtyard, and when they entered the door of his home he closed it behind them. Tor-yonah was left outside to wait. And wait. And wait.

When the sun burned persimmon in the western sky and the door was still not opened, Tor-yonah became anxious. He knew the Young Mother was ever protective of the Child, and he instinctively knew that the kinsman's wife, the Laughing One, mothered all who entered her home, but he could not tolerate this separation. He flew to the small windows, trying to peer inside, but shades of oiled parchment had been hung there, and he could see nothing. At last he

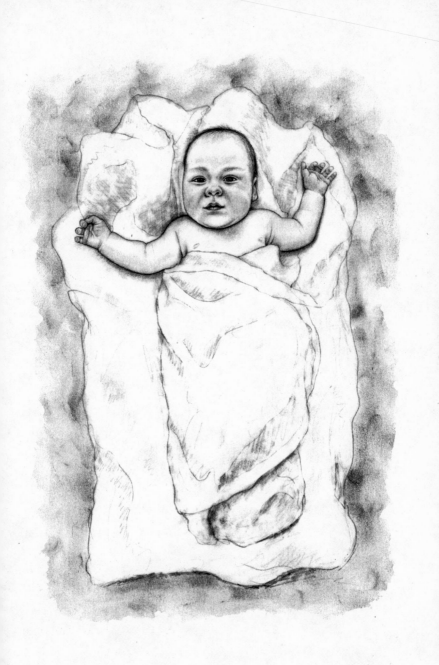

found a small window where the covering had been pulled aside.

The baby lay on the floor amid brightly covered pillows. The two families sat on pillows at a low table. The eldest son was lighting a taper, and Tor-yonah heard him whisper, "Adonai."

At the moment the holy name was uttered, the baby looked up at Tor-yonah. Dimples about the small mouth deepened, and the rosy lips curled upward.

The Child had smiled at him! All was well. He flew to the rooftop to wait.

As he waited, he tried to push aside the warnings—the danger—that continued to alarm him. Each time his fears for the Child had been unfounded, yet he believed there must be some reason for his concern. Did these feelings come from some source outside of himself? He couldn't know that not many days would pass until he understood the reasons for his foreboding.

One day, with the donkey, Tor-yonah and the family went into the city to market. There were plenty of fish and fowl at the river, but they planned to buy fruit, grain, and vegetables. And they looked forward to a holiday.

Tor-yonah perched upon the Young Mother's shoulder, enjoying the sights of the marketplace. There were great throngs of people in the city. Tor-yonah soon realized that these people had come for a special day of worship. Crowds lined the streets, straining for a glimpse of something— some distant person or object coming toward them.

The Tall One and the Young Mother paused in curiosity. Tor-yonah became anxious, for it was evident the people were on the verge of hysteria as the object of their interest drew near. The Mother held her baby close in an effort to protect him from the teeming crowds. When heralding instruments burst forth, many of the onlookers fell to the dust, screaming and writhing. Soldiers struggled to hold back the surging mass.

Tor-yonah flew above the crowds, looking for the source of this frenzy. He was amazed at what he saw.

An awesome spectacle met his eyes. A throne

was being carried by four men. The throne and the carved idol seated upon it were the color of the sun, but the tones were richer—like the gifts brought to the Child. The golden head was that of a falcon, the body was that of a man. The Falcon-Man held a sun disk in his hands.

When the procession passed where the family stood, many fell prostrate before him.

A man shouted, "Our Radiance, the God of Sun!"

And a woman fell to the dirt, her hands uplifted, beseeching.

"Never leave us, O Ra, for we will die without your warmth and light!"

"These people are pagans!" the Tall One said to his wife. "They are worshiping a graven image! They are breaking the commandments!"

The Young Mother gently tugged at his robe. Her reply was soft amid the noise and confusion. The Tall One had to bend to hear her words.

"They do not know the one true God, Husband."

(At one time Ra had been the first god in the land of the pharaohs. Now there were many gods, and this idol was but one of them.)

Without warning, a man Tor-yonah had seen at the temple of the Most High burst forth from the crowd. Tor-yonah had heard that this man was from their native land. The man was wild—possessed by demons. His clothes were ragged and dirty, his hair a tangled mass of oily brown about his face. In his insanity he had turned against the God of his fathers.

"Stop!" the Tormented One screeched to the men who carried the throne.

To Tor-yonah's surprise, the men stopped. Then the dove remembered the kinsman's telling of a law that declared that any citizen was allowed to ask a yes-or-no question of a god carried in a procession. If a symbolic event occurred, this was considered an answer from the god.

The man ran backward before the procession.

"Listen to me, O golden man-bird! Am I to worship you or the God of my fathers?"

A soldier rushed forward with uplifted sword.

"Stupid madman! You have insulted His Radiance! You shall die!"

"Kill him! Kill him!" was the raging cry of the crowd.

Tor-yonah knew he must not let this terrible thing happen. The soldier was poised to drive his sword into the man's heart, but Tor-yonah flew before the soldier's face, flapping wildly. A symbolic event! The crowd gasped!

The soldier fell to the ground. His fear made him as stone.

With a mighty leap the Tormented One threw himself upon the dove and clasped him with massive hands, but Tor-yonah could see the Tall One running after him.

The crazed man was too swift! Tor-yonah was jolted over uneven streets and alleys. The man's tight grasp was stealing his breath. Then terror overwhelmed him, and he gave in to engulfing blackness.

Chapter Four

Tor-yonah looked sadly through the reed bars of a cage held together by a mud-hardened floor and ceiling. The area was small, scarcely large enough for his body, with little space for movement. He was on the ground outside a striped tent, and the river was nearby. When he turned his head, he saw three pyramids and the large angular likeness of a man's head. He must be south of the ancient fig tree on the western side of the river. He had seen these great monuments when he had flown above the caravan.

A sound came from the tent, and Tor-yonah turned, expecting to see the man. A small boy emerged, ragged and filthy as the man. Dark curls tangled around his small, pinched face. His eyes were large and brown. For a fleeting instant when he saw Tor-yonah, the dullness in them disappeared.

"A dove!" he exclaimed. "Is he for me?"

He reached hesitantly into the cage. Tor-yonah wanted his comforting touch, but it was not to be. The raucous voice of the Tormented One burst forth.

"Stupid child! Don't you dare to touch him! He is sacred. You will defile him!"

"Then how did he get here? Didn't you have to touch him?"

The Tormented One's face was cruel in anger. He grasped a large stick from the ground, lunged at the boy, and missed. Nimbly, the boy ran toward the river.

"Hah!" the man cried. "You question your father? Impudent viper! Come here to me! The sacred scrolls say I should use the rod on you, and by all that is holy, I will!"

Tor-yonah could see the boy darting from palm tree to palm tree.

The man spun about.

"Ra-a-hrr!" he growled, falling to the ground by Tor-yonah's cage. He seemed to be bowing, the way people had bowed to the Falcon-Man.

"You're a god, aren't you?" he asked, then talked to the dove in the manner that Tor-yonah's family had talked to Yahweh. "Oh, dove, if you *are*, restore a right spirit within me!"

Suddenly the man leaped into the air. "You're no god!" he shrieked. His fingers twisted and stretched toward the heavens.

His whisper was hoarse, "Where are you, Yahweh? Are you in the mountains of my boyhood home? Are you in the desert? Are you with the dead in their great tombs in this strange land? Are you in the river?"

He became quiet, but a cunning look was in his eyes.

"You are not in the carved gods of these people, are you? Aha! The little dove fooled the people, didn't he?"

He fell to the ground again, writhing and shaking. Foam bubbled on his lips. Finally spent, he lay still. Then his eyes opened. He rolled to his stomach, his face level with the cage.

"Why did you flap your wings before the soldier's eyes? Is there something sacred about you? All doves have eyes of peace that seem to look into the soul, but you . . . Listen! I will tell you something. I have deceived the people in this land too. They think I am an oracle. I tell them what they want to hear. I pretend to worship their gods and the gods of their conquerors. But perhaps you . . ." His eyes narrowed. "*Are* you a god?"

In his desire to respond, Tor-yonah began the instinctive motion of flight. The movement startled the man, who sprang to a crouching position.

"A-agh! Of course you're no god! I need no god!"

Leaping up, he kicked at the cage but missed. Furious with frustration, he raged into the tent. When he came out, a large sack was in his hands. Tor-yonah thought that the sack was intended for him, but the man walked past the cage without a glance. He did not appear again until the sun had slipped behind the pyramids.

Time passed slowly for the dove. His days were spent watching his captor and the boy. Sometimes the man made small gestures of kindness to his son, but more often the boy was beaten. Tor-yonah ached to console the unhappy child.

Five full moons had shone upon the great stone monuments since his capture. Where was his family! Were they still beneath the fig tree? Had they returned to the hill country of their homeland? Surely they would stay in this land as long as the evil king ruled their province. If he could get free, he would fly in search of them.

Then he had the dream.

In this dream he saw himself with the Child. But the Child had become a man. A radiant light was shining, and there was the sound of a mighty voice. The voice of Yahweh? In hazy dream-confusion he was uncertain. Did Yahweh have plans for the birds of the air as well as man? Surely not the same kinds of plans. He would not forget the dream.

Each day the Tormented One left with his sack. In the evening he returned with food and objects of value. Tor-yonah decided that the man must go with these objects to the City of the Sun for silver or trading.

When the man was away, the boy talked for long hours to the dove.

"Do you know, dove, it will soon be time for us to move away from the river? The gods from the south send a flood of water that covers the land on either side to bring forth harvest. It is called the *inundation.*"

Will my family know of the inundation? Tor-yonah asked himself.

"Greetings, dove. I caught a very big fish in the river today. Maybe my father will be proud of me."

How can the man be cruel to this boy? thought Tor-yonah.

"Dove, my father says I killed my mother by being born. I wonder how I could have killed her. I don't remember it at all. I must be an evil boy to have killed my mother."

Is this the reason for the man's madness? Tor-yonah wondered.

"Dove, isn't it strange that I love my father and hate him too? Will the gods punish me for that?"

One day the boy untied the leather thongs to the cage door.

"I love you, little dove," he whispered. "I want to hold you. If I were a big man, I'd catch my father in a snare and cage him as he is caging you."

Tor-yonah wanted to feel the love in the boy's hands. Even more, he wanted to be free. But he was not allowed to make this decision. He couldn't understand why he had not seen the man coming; the earth was flat for many miles around their area of the river. The screeching suddenness of him filled Tor-yonah with terror.

The crazed man grabbed the cage and flung his son to the ground. He fumbled with the thongs, attempting to tie them. When he could not, he grasped the cage with both hands and threw it with force. Over and over it turned, Tor-yonah tumbling with it. It came to rest at the trunk of a palm tree.

Tor-yonah was motionless with shock until he realized he was unhurt. The reeds to his cage were broken and part of the mud flooring had fallen away. He walked out of the brokenness and onto the grass. His feathers twisted into a downstroke as he prepared for flight. The man saw but he was too far away. The dove was free!

Tor-yonah's impulse was to fly away, but for some reason he could not. He wanted to leave—to soar into the air, to be free of the Tormented One, free of the cage. Free of the boy? No. He had not realized until this moment that he loved the boy. And in disbelief he knew that he cared also for the Tormented One. He flew about the man, flapping his wings wildly. The man was as bewildered as the dove. His breath caught, and he cringed in fear as Tor-yonah landed on his shoulder. The boy, amazed at this, ran toward them, but something stopped him. He became as a statue, his eyes widened with uncertainty.

Some Force had stopped Tor-yonah. And this

same Power seemed to affect all their surroundings. A stillness came upon the earth. All was quiet. Nothing moved—not the date palms—not the tamarisk trees—not the reeds by the river—not the man—not Tor-yonah. Sitting there on the man's shoulder, he was as still as the ancient monuments on the horizon.

There was a rushing noise then, like the fluttering wings of a thousand doves. The sound drew near and surrounded them, and a hurling blast of wind swept across the place where they stood. The trees bent with the force of it, and a choking dust swirled about them. Tor-yonah flailed against the strength of it with his wings, and the boy was forced to the ground. Suddenly the dove felt the man's protective hand encircling him. As the man fell to his knees, he reached out for the boy. The wind swirled over them, and they clung together in fear. They watched as it swept across the face of the river.

The Presence left as quickly as it had come. When all was over, the man continued to hold the boy and the dove.

Stunned, he said, "My soul is at peace. . . ."

He stood then, his arm around the boy's shoulder, holding him close. The hand that held Tor-yonah was lifted high.

He looked up at Tor-yonah. Slowly, gently, he opened his fingers.

"Was it the wind?" he whispered. "Were you in the wind? You have healed me, dove. Go where you will."

What had happened? The man believed Tor-yonah had driven out the evil demons that had possessed him, but the dove knew he'd had nothing to do with it. There had been a miracle in the wind.

Tor-yonah paused only for a moment. He saw the boy's eyes, and he knew it was all right to leave.

Chapter Five

He had almost forgotten the joy of flight, the exhilaration of wind through his wingtips, the gliding smoothness of the strong up-and-down strokes. He had almost forgotten the rapture of height, the curve of the great earth beneath him.

He had not forgotten the Child.

Using the sun for navigation, he flew first to the fig tree. His gaze swept across the vast stretches of land. His family was no longer there, the mud hut that had housed the carpenter's tools was empty, and the tent was gone.

What should he do? If he flew along the caravan route and they were retracing their travels, he would find them easily. Would they return to the place of the Child's birth if the evil king still reigned?

The kinsman! His family had gone to stay with the kinsman! He lost no time flying to the City of the Sun to find them.

All through the afternoon he circled their home, and when none of the family ventured outside or to the courtyard, he spent the night on their rooftop.

Early, when the first rooster crowed, the eldest son and one of his younger brothers came out carrying water jars. The dove flew about their hands, hoping to be noticed. After a short while the younger child placed his jug on the ground and pointed.

"Look, brother!" he cried. "Isn't that the dove who came with our cousins?"

"I think you're right," the older boy said. "Poor dove. Our cousin said he was stolen by the

Tormented One who begs at the temple of the Most High. He must have escaped."

"Let's get a snare," the younger child said.

Tor-yonah flew to the farthest corner of the house—to the stone arch that decorated the rooftop. He must not risk being captured again, even by this good family.

I will come to them only if the Child is here, he decided.

The Laughing One was called, and she came out, her cupped hands full of seeds. Tor-yonah was happy to see her again, but he looked toward the door, hoping for a glimpse of the Young Mother holding the Child.

The Laughing One said, "He only stares at us. Come, Tor-yonah, we're your friends."

Yes, but please, I want only to know about my family, Tor-yonah cried out silently.

"Get your father," the Laughing One said to her sons.

The kinsman's hair shone a bright red-orange in the sunlight.

"Tor-yonah!" he boomed. "Come down to us! Your family has returned to their home. You'll never find them now. You are too domesticated to live in the wilds."

That, O kinsman, is what I wished to know, the dove thought to himself.

"He cocks his head as if he understands," the Laughing One said, "and have you noticed? We all talk to that dove as if he were human."

"I don't know what he is," the kinsman said, shaking his head, "but my cousin's gentle wife thought he understood, and maybe she was right!"

Tor-yonah was sad to leave them, but depart he must. On impulse he flew to the courtyard, straight as a bee returning to its hive. After swooping in a tight circle about them, he sailed with purpose into the skies. Then he flew east toward the route of the caravan, to the paths he had traveled months before with his family. His years of search had begun.

No zealot ever gave of himself with more resolve. He would find the Child—his reason for being.

When he sighted travelers along the highways, he swooped down to listen and look. Could the Child be among them?

At the Great Sea he landed on the bow of a beached fishing vessel where fishermen were mending their nets. One of them spoke in fearful tones to another.

"We must be careful in the provinces to the southeast," he said. "When the evil king died, I had great hopes, but his son is now governor of three provinces, and I hear the son is as ruthless as his father."

Where did my family go when they heard that news? pondered Tor-yonah.

He flew over great stretches of land, stopping only to glean information or to find food. He sought them in the wilderness of Shur and on the plains of Philistia. He swooped low over the Sea of the Plain. He searched for them as he traversed the mountains of Shephelah and the plains of Sharon. He looked for them as he flew over Mount Carmel and the brook of Kidron. He returned to the City of David, but the family had not returned to the Child's birthplace. Always he was disappointed.

He remembered the Young Mother and the Tall One speaking of their hometown. When they lived on the flat deserts by the Blue River, the girl had spoken of those hills. Had they returned? The Tall One said he'd lived a short distance from a lake called the Sea of the Garden. He would go there.

He found the Town of the Branch and the Tall One's carpenter father. The Tall One's mother must have gone to rest with Abraham, for the old man lived alone in his house. He seldom looked up from the furniture he was shaping with a cutting tool. Tor-yonah watched the man for several days.

One day when the dove's wings caused a whispery rustle amid the leaves of the tamarisk tree, the old carpenter peered through the branches.

"Say, little bird, are you wounded? Why do you stay here with me? Come. Let me see."

Tor-yonah flew to a higher limb and hid himself among the pink blossoms.

"Ah, so you're all right? That's good," the carpenter murmured, and he returned to his work.

I will never learn about the family from this busy man, the dove thought.

Then a young man came into the shed to work with the old carpenter, and Tor-yonah listened.

"Have you heard from your son and his wife?" the young man asked. "It is long since they went to be taxed in David's city."

The old carpenter shook his head in sorrow.

"No. No one has heard from them. I fear they have met with evil. If they are still alive, I pray the Lord God to protect them."

Tor-yonah didn't wait. He had heard all he needed to hear.

And so, over the years he continued his search. Without the Child he was incomplete. Success was never with him, but he would not stop searching. He joined the migrations of other doves, always watching, filled with longing. Once they flew to the land of the pharaohs, south where the mighty monsoons flooded the river and caused its yearly inundation, but Tor-yonah soon returned; he was sure his family had not made their home there.

Then one spring in the land of his birth, he flew over a long caravan returning from its stay in the Holy City. He scanned each face, looking, searching, hoping. . . . It was useless. He circled to leave, but when he turned and banked, he saw the man, the Tall One! Praise be to Yahweh! He could not be mistaken! The man had changed somewhat. His hair had silvered at his forehead; there were lines about his mouth and eyes. But he would know this man anywhere!

The Young Mother and the Child must be nearby! Now the pain would be gone—the hunger and thirst would be satisfied. With joy he left the other doves and descended. But in mid-flight his thinking changed.

No. I must not come upon them like this. So much time has passed since they last saw me. They may not remember.

He flew lower, careful to keep himself hidden. There was the Young Mother—no longer a girl. A lovely woman now. The Mother of the Child!

He landed close by, careful to keep out of

sight. He learned they were returning from the Holy City, where they had taken part in the Feast of the Unleavened Bread.

But where was the Child? He flew overhead, scanning the caravan. The family was here and the Child must surely be with them! When he saw the Child, Tor-yonah would make himself known to him and would stay with him forever.

But something was wrong. The parents were troubled. He moved closer and heard the man speaking to another member of the caravan.

"We'll try to join you later. We're heartsore with worry. We thought our son to be with friends; he had stayed with their children on our journey to the city. He was with us at the feast, and we had thought he would be with them on our return. But now they say he didn't join them as they'd expected. They thought he was with us."

Tor-yonah was cold with fear. He had searched for so long, and now . . . He could not bear it if something had happened to the Child. Had he found them too late?

He followed as they anxiously inquired of friends and acquaintances in the city. The Child had not been seen. They went to the temple to ask his whereabouts of the learned men who came each day to discuss the questions of life. The men were there, and a young man was with them.

Why, it was . . . Yes, it must be—it *was*—the Child! Tor-yonah knew with certainty when the Mother and the Tall One both cried out in relief!

He was overjoyed. He would swoop down and land upon the young man's shoulder! He would make himself known! But he was suddenly overcome with awe.

How foolish I have been. I haven't looked for a young man; I thought of him as a child. He must be twelve by now; we're the same age. Tor-yonah reproached himself.

He perched, hidden behind the leaves of the terebinth tree in the courtyard, puzzled by this strange shyness that had overtaken him.

The Mother scolded her son in the soft tones of a woman. "Son! Why have you done this to us? We have been sorrowing with fear!"

The young man looked at her with a question in his eyes.

"Why did you need to look?" he said. "Didn't you know I must be about my Father's business?"

His Father's business! He does not mean the Tall One! He means Yahweh! I should have known! This is Yahweh's own Son!

He wanted to go to the Child. How wonderful to be with him again! But he knew he must not show himself now. With a startling clarity he realized that all creatures were of Yahweh, and this meant there was a plan for his life too. Had not the Young Mother once said that even sparrows were shielded by the wings of the Most High?

The Child lifted his head and saw the dove among the leaves of the terebinth tree. Their eyes met, and Tor-yonah knew the bond was unbroken. Joy and sorrow were intertwined as surely as the clinging vine laces through the limbs of a tree. With regret he lifted his wings and soared into the waiting skies. He too must be about the Father's business.

Chapter Six

Tor-yonah decided to yield himself to Yahweh's will, for he wished to understand what "his Father's business" meant for him. He soon knew. Yahweh led him across the plains, through mountain passes, and around and about the cities. He found himself in the company of kings and judges, princes and governors in need of Yahweh's wisdom and strength. He was drawn to these people as if by some magnetic pull. As in the past with the Tormented One and the boy, a Presence had come at the moment of their needs, and he came to know that Presence as *Neshemah*.

Neshemah! The Holy Spirit! He recalled words he had heard the Young Mother and the Tall One say about a Spirit that had visited them both. The Spirit had come in different forms, sometimes in a brilliant light—sometimes in the still, small voice of Yahweh. Sometimes in the wind.

The wind! He remembered the wind that had arisen the day the man had been healed of his demons, and he knew the truth. *Neshemah had been in that wind!*

In those years before he had found the Child in the temple, he thought that his reason for being was to be with the Child. Now he believed there was some service he was to perform. Was this to be for Neshemah? For Yahweh? For the Child?

He was a dove with seriousness of purpose, but he also knew love and lightness of heart. Flying through the mountains he would sing, *El Shaddai.* As he realized the fullness of Yahweh's deity, he sang, *Elohim, Elohim.* And because he had come to know Yahweh as a God of vision, he sang, *El Roi, El Roi, El Roi.*

In the twenty-ninth year of Tor-yonah's life, he was drawn to a governor's palace. He stopped to rest in the garden, a place of oleanders, lilies, and willows, with a small brook curving among the graceful trees. There he perched among the lacy branches of a willow and there he came to know the girl child.

Above the burbling of the brook Tor-yonah heard a soft moan. Through the slender leaves he saw that a pallet had been placed on the grass. A small girl lay upon it. Her stifled sobs filled Tor-yonah with compassion. As he watched, a servant woman came out with a bowl of broth.

"Please, little one, you must eat," the woman said.

Pale hair fell about the girl's pillow and framed an equally pale face. Her eyes mirrored the blue of the skies, but they were listless.

All afternoon Tor-yonah watched the little one, and late in the day her father, the governor, came from his work to sit by his daughter. His wife soon joined them in the garden. As she knelt by the pallet, the woman's drawn face told Tor-yonah that the girl had been ill for a long time.

He lifted his wings and flew to the ground, where he perched on a rock near the girl's head. For the first time in his afternoon vigil, she smiled.

"Look, Father. Mother, look! This little dove isn't afraid of me."

The mother and the father were pleased to see their daughter's smile. Delighted, the mother stepped forward, but the father placed a restraining hand on her arm. "Shh, we'll frighten him away."

Each noonday the little girl was brought out to the garden. Her physicians believed the warmth of the sun might strengthen her, but nothing seemed to help. Every day Tor-yonah hopped down to be near her. Her parents and the servants were amazed to see the smile upon the girl's face.

The governor said to his wife, "It's a strange thing, but our daughter takes sustenance now that the dove has come, and I believe she's growing stronger."

But somehow Tor-yonah felt there was no hope for the girl child.

I will stay nearby to give her comfort in these last days, he promised himself.

When they were alone, the girl whispered to him in a voice so low that he could scarcely hear, "I will be leaving my mother and father soon, little bird. I don't want to go, but the angel of death is calling me."

Tor-yonah lifted his wings and flew to the first branches of the willow; perhaps she would enjoy the sunset color of his underwings. He was right, because she softly exclaimed, "Ah, you are so pretty, little dove! Please don't ever leave me."

He decided he would stay as long as the girl needed him, but in a few days something happened that distressed him gravely. Having come to recognize the drawing power of Neshemah, obedience had become an instinct. He felt the urgent force of the Spirit and knew he was being called to fulfill his purpose. The pull of duty was powerful, and he was in terror of that unknown duty that beckoned him. But he wished to stay with the girl.

Perhaps it would be all right to ignore the Spirit. Only a small bird, he *had* made the girl child happy. Then Tor-yonah realized the truth: He had received joy and contentment in return. He could not leave her.

He had spent many years obeying the Spirit. Surely it would not be wrong to give in to his own pleasures at this time of his life. And were not his reasons unselfish? The girl child was more joyful because of him. He saw her eyes searching for him amid the willow leaves each day. He watched her pleased smile when he flew down to the flowering bush by her side. When he was there, she would drink the broth prepared by the servants. And now it seemed that he could see a slight pink in her cheeks, a clearer blue in her eyes. Neshemah would understand. Was this not the Father's business? He would stay with her until she went to be with Abraham and Sarah.

But one day as he watched her sleeping, the presence of the Spirit was overpowering, and he knew he could no longer disobey. He did not know how he could leave; the pain of separation was unbearable. His happiness was with the little girl, but his duty was with the Spirit. And although the decision came with clarity, the reasons were unclear as they had been from the beginning.

He flew down to her, wishing he could speak the language of humans. He wanted so desperately for her to understand. He was gladdened when she reached out and encircled him with frail hands, her slender fingers as light and fluttering as butterflies.

"Mother! Father! Come see!" she called in soft, treble tones.

Her father and mother rushed out to see the cause of the girl's cry, but they stopped in terror. A black cloud had suddenly covered the sky above them and reached down into the garden. In a moment day became night, and low, ominous thunder rumbled into a roar.

Then an exciting thing happened. In joy the girl leaped up. As she did, she released Tor-yonah, and the cloud disappeared. The sky was silken blue, and a radiant shaft of sunlight surrounded her. She raised eager arms to her father and mother. Tor-yonah saw her pink cheeks, her joyful eyes. She was well! He knew it! *Neshemah had been in the thunder.*

Tor-yonah lifted and soared into the heavens. He had chosen to obey the Father, and the Spirit had made it possible for him to go.

Chapter Seven

Tor-yonah felt himself propelled by a terrible and relentless Force. Even the movement of his wings seemed to come from outside his own will. Flying with unaccustomed speed, he experienced a feeling close to terror when he realized he could neither stop nor change his course.

Then the fearsome Power released its hold, and the dove was able to glide freely to a tree overlooking a river. A morning sun gleamed across the face of the water, turning it into a glimmering brightness. Many men lined its shores. With great interest the crowd was watching two men who were standing in the river. He could see that an unusual event was taking place.

Each man was a marvelous sight to behold. One wore a leather girdle about his waist and a cloak of camel's hair. He was lean and muscular of body, and his skin was brown and lined from the sun and wind. The brown of the reeds was the color of his hair, streaked with the sun's gold. Tor-yonah heard the men along the shore speak of this man as the Prophet Proclaimer.

The other man was even more compelling than the prophet. Tor-yonah sensed this but was uncertain of the reason. This man too was strong—a man accustomed to labor and the elements. His clothes were not unusual, but there was something different about him. A strength and dignity. A beauty of spirit. And yes, a mystical aura—something Tor-yonah had seen in no other man.

The dove flew from the tree and hovered above the two men, watching and listening. The prophet placed his arm in a supporting position

behind the man's back. Tor-yonah surmised that the prophet was going to immerse the man in the sacred rite of baptism.

As the man was lowered into the water, his eyes met the eyes of Tor-yonah, and the dove knew! This was the Child! The one to whom he was bonded. Of course! He was a man now!

This is the fulfillment of the dream! This is the day I have lived for! This is Yahweh's plan!

He felt he could not contain the glorious happiness of it! Exultantly he sailed into the skies. In joy he gave himself to the Spirit's guidance, and he was surrounded by Neshemah. The Spirit was around, above, and within him.

A shaft of pure light encircled Tor-yonah, and Neshemah led him to the man.

"You are Yahweh's Son," Tor-yonah sang, but his words were the words of Neshemah, heard only with the heart.

The man whispered, "Tor-yonah." And around and above and within Tor-yonah was a voice. Yahweh's? The voice was like a song, and the spoken words had the beauty and sweetness of music.

"This is my Son whom I love; I am delighted with him."

Tor-yonah became aware of amazement in the eyes of the crowd. The people were staring at *him!* What did they see? He looked into the water at his reflection, and he could not believe the image there! His feathers were no longer pastel. His feathers were pure white.

A shimmering light encircled him. In ecstasy he realized the beautiful truth. Yahweh had chosen *him,* a mere dove, as his symbol for the Unseen Spirit.

In that moment Tor-yonah knew that nothing would ever again separate him from *this* Man! The One to whom he was bonded.

Broadmoor Books of Zondervan Publishing House is quite proud
to offer this special Christmas story to your family.
It is our hope that the love and care that went
into the production of this volume will
result in this book's being enjoyed
year after year as part of your
family's Advent celebration.
We hope that it will
be a warm reminder
of the reason
we celebrate
Christmas.

Illustrator—Catherine Reishus McLaughlin. Cover
design—Terry Dugan. Compositor—
Susan Koppenol. Editors—
Mary McCormick and
Bob Hudson.